Be brave! Enjoy your journey

Dedicated to the children of the Gulf Coast... and beyond.

Goldie's Search for SILVER

by
Timothy A. Weeks

illustrated by
Miss Jeanne & Miss Lala

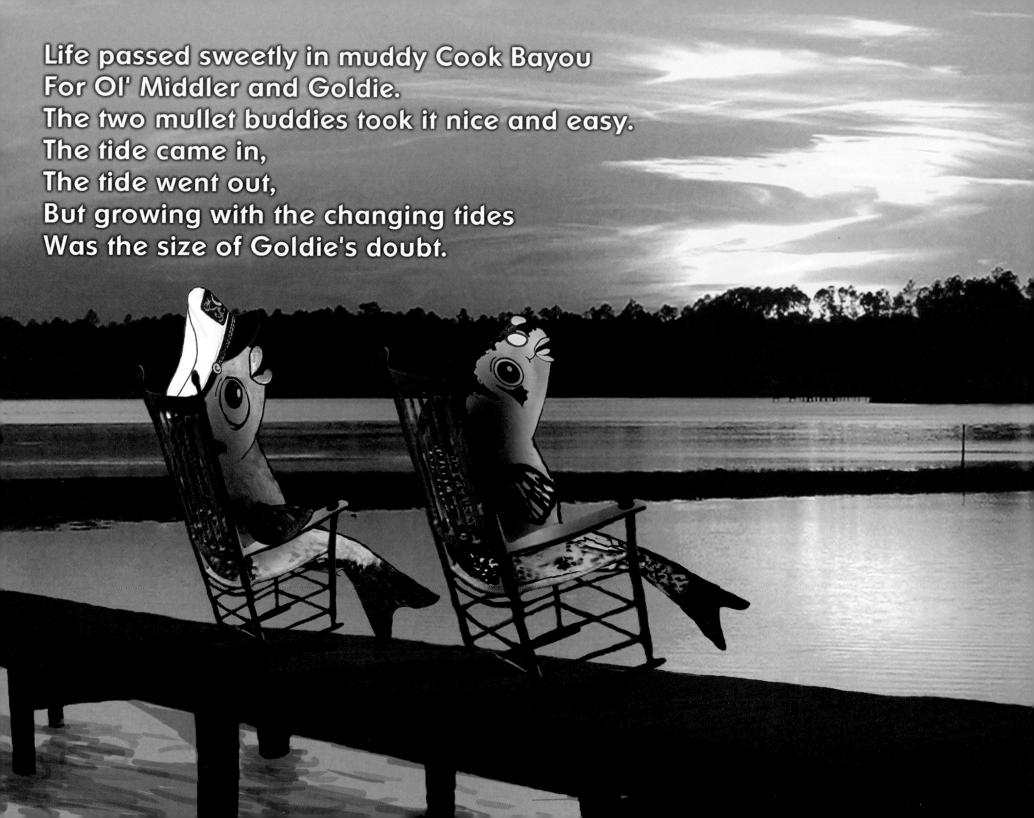

Life passed sweetly in muddy Cook Bayou
For Ol' Middler and Goldie.
The two mullet buddies took it nice and easy.
The tide came in,
The tide went out,
But growing with the changing tides
Was the size of Goldie's doubt.

For Goldie missed Silver dearly.
His precious, precious Silver,
Who on that nightmare of a day,
Had been swept away
By the awful hurricane.

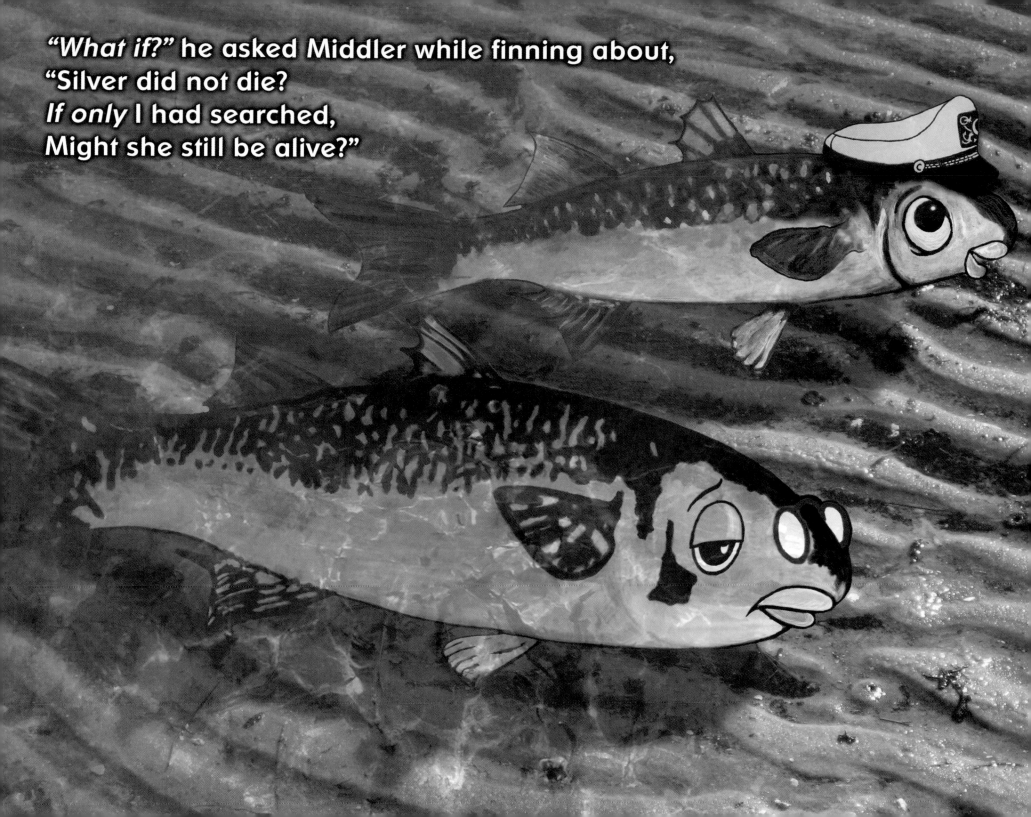

"*What if?*" he asked Middler while finning about,
"Silver did not die?
If only I had searched,
Might she still be alive?"

Ol' Middler lifted his cap
With his right fin,
And scratched his scaly noggin
With his left.
"I'm a simple mullet, Goldie.
I don't know much
About philosophy and such,
But it's not good to feel guilty
About what you *can't* change,
Only about what you *won't*."

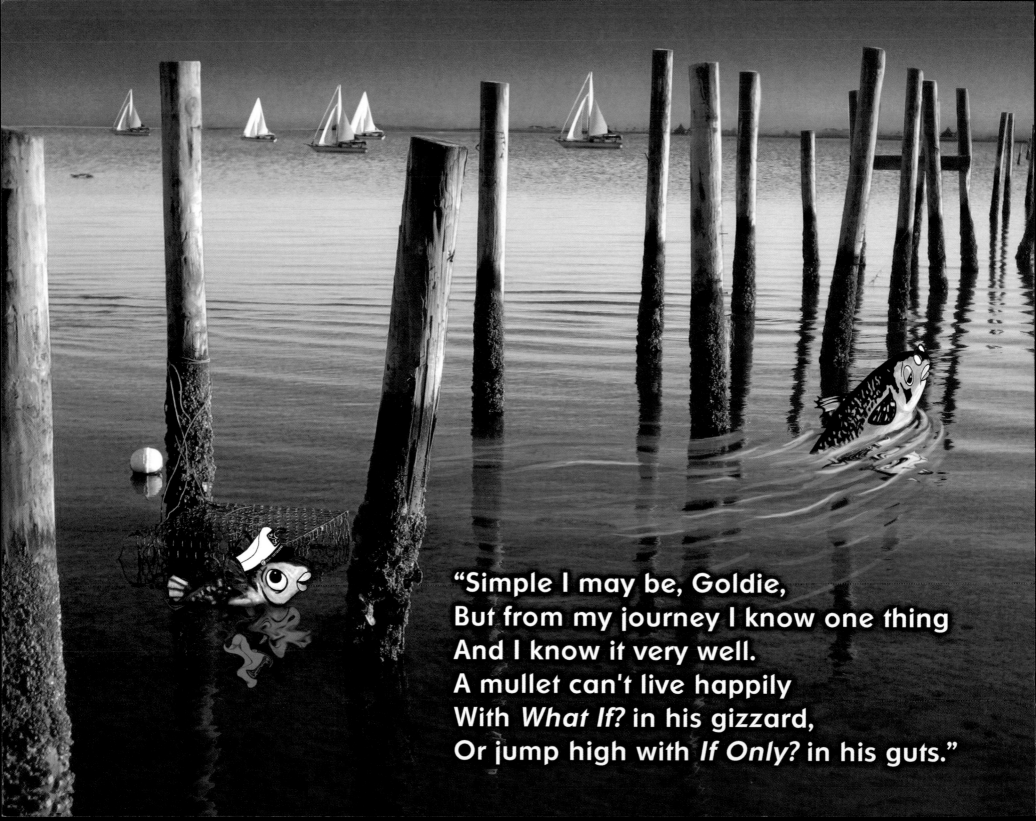

"Simple I may be, Goldie,
But from my journey I know one thing
And I know it very well.
A mullet can't live happily
With *What If?* in his gizzard,
Or jump high with *If Only?* in his guts."

Did I do all I could? wondered Goldie
Under the starry Cook Bayou sky.
Have I done all I should?
And if not, why?

Disaster struck at dawn,
While Middler and Goldie fed with the rising tide.
An osprey swooped down,

And scooped Ol' Middler up.

How Goldie grieved for his loyal buddy!
There had never been a better friend.
Saluting Ol' Middler,
He wiped a tear from his eye,
And departed Cook Bayou
For the very last time.

There would be no more *What Ifs,*
No more sitting on his fins.
Goldie had made up his mind:
I will find my precious Silver,
Or spend my life trying.

He searched Boggy Bayou,
Pensacola, Mobile Bay,
Dauphin Island, Horn Island,
Intracoastal Waterway,
Santa Rosa, Pascagoula,
Perdido Key,
Florida, Alabama,
All the way to Mississippi.

Goldie searched day and night
For weeks and months.
Seasons passed,
But Silver remained lost.

Lost but alive,
Silver had survived
The awful storm,
While many creatures died.

But just when she was
Feeling a little less poorly,

Another hurricane struck!

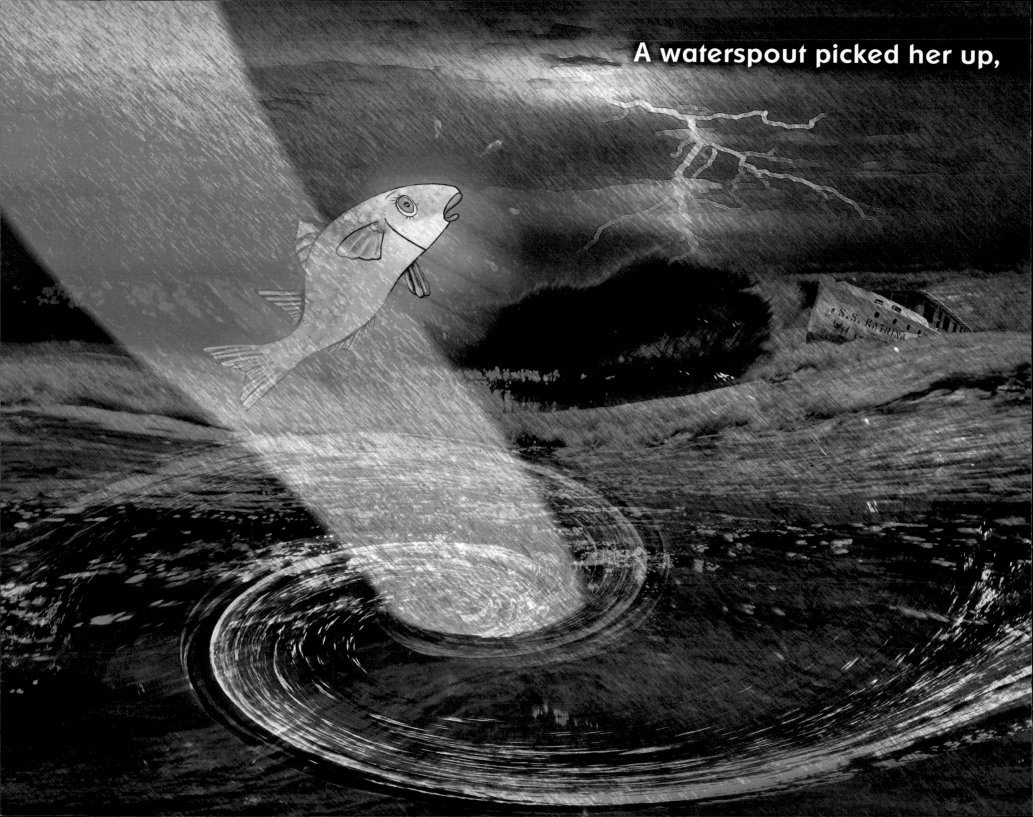

A waterspout picked her up,

And dropped her down
In a Cajun cypress swamp,
With a fractured fin
And a broken heart.

Battered, bruised, broken – alone and so lonely,
Far from Pretty Bayou
With no sign of Goldie.

The sparkle faded from Silver's blue eyes.
The dazzle departed her hoppy tail.
And her once shiny scales,
Those shiniest of scales,
Now looked like crinkled aluminum foil.

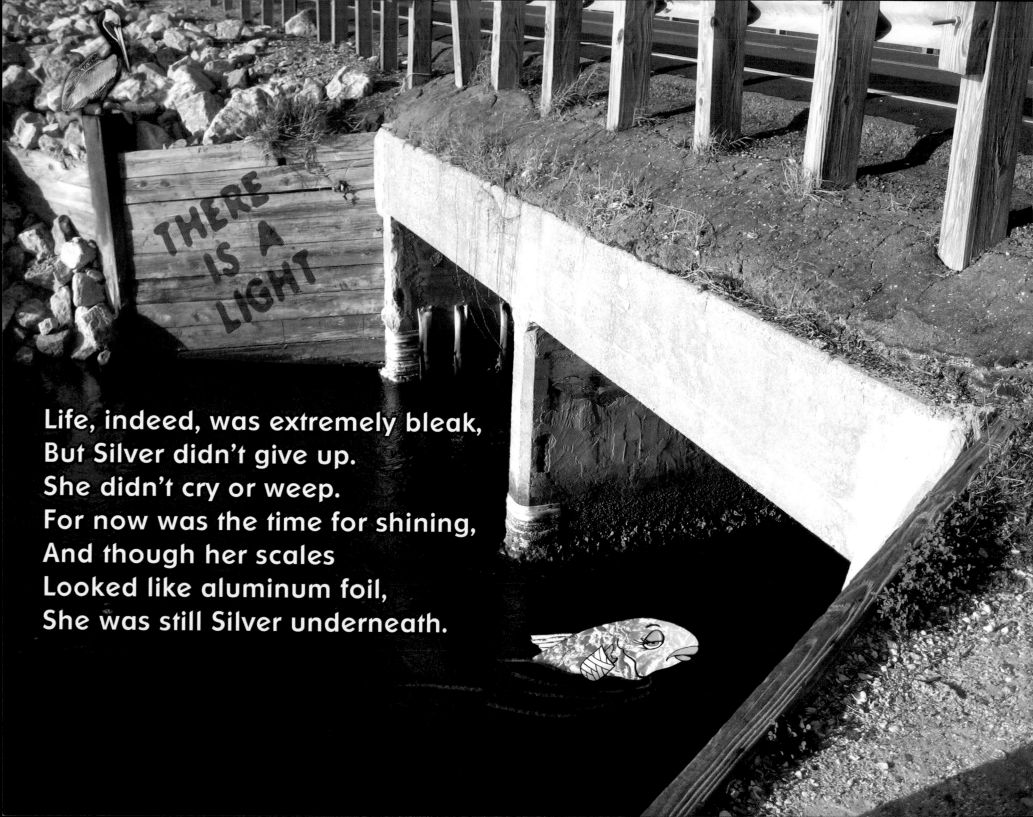

THERE
IS A
LIGHT

Life, indeed, was extremely bleak,
But Silver didn't give up.
She didn't cry or weep.
For now was the time for shining,
And though her scales
Looked like aluminum foil,
She was still Silver underneath.

That never goes out

She struggled.
She half-swam.
She paddled slowly along,
Looking for Goldie
And longing for home.

Alligators,

Gars,
Ospreys and snakes,
Silver dodged dangers
However they came.

Until one magical morning,
Silver's perseverance paid off.
She saw red glasses on the horizon
And something golden wagging.
Suddenly her scales were shining,
For she knew
Her Goldie was coming.

But just at the moment she started to wave,
At the instant she started to shout,
A wily Cajun threw a castnet over her head
And pulled her onto his dock.

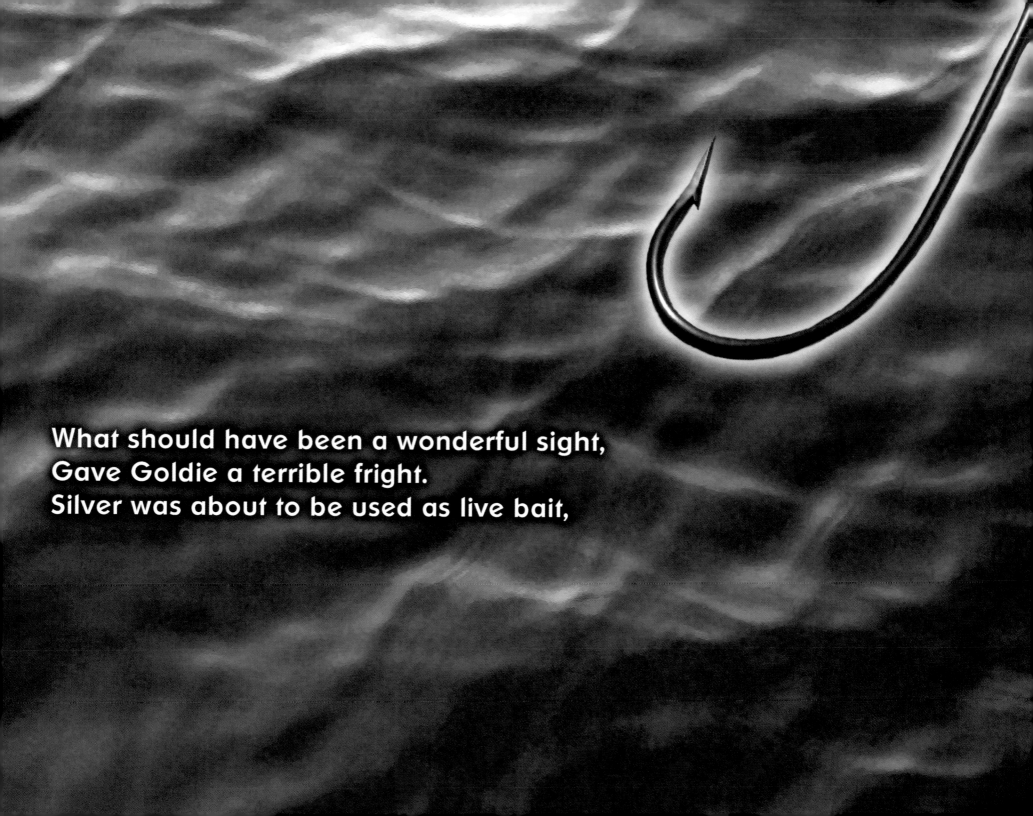

What should have been a wonderful sight,
Gave Goldie a terrible fright.
Silver was about to be used as live bait,

To catch a Big **Bull** Red!

There was no time to worry,
No time to despair.
His little voice said *Swim Fast!*
And then it hollared *Jump!*

How high did Goldie jump that fateful day?
Well in Terrebonne Parish the old-timers say,
"*Choo!* he jumped *beaucoup* high!
The fust time evuh a mullet did fly!"

NO WAY ZONE

High, high, high, Goldie soared in the sky,
Higher than a mullet was supposed to be.
He smacked into that Cajun's hand,
And knocked his Silver free!

No time to celebrate,
No time to hug,
They jumped together
Just as the big redfish struck!

They swam like the dickens
And hid up a slough.
And then, only then,
Silver said,
"You sure took your time.
But *boy*, am I glad to see you."

It was a morning like none other.
And to celebrate their reunion
Silver said, "Let's return to Pretty Bayou
By taking the scenic route."

Louisiana, Texas, Mexico,
Across to the Florida Keys,
They traveled like it was their honeymoon
And did just as they pleased.

ATLANTIC
OCEAN

Bahamas

Cuba

Haiti

Jamaica

Greetings from Morgan City!

Wish you were here!
Goldie & Silver

They springed in Morgan City,

And summered in Cancun,

They autumned in the Everglades,
And wintered by Cedar Key.

And everywhere they went,
They never traveled alone.
Because everywhere they went,
The memory of his loyal buddy
Traveled with Goldie too.

They traveled so long
Goldie got to feeling his age.
He wasn't a buck mullet.
His bones were tired.
His jumping days were nearly over.
His scales constantly ached.

Silver noticed and slowed her pace.
Then she stopped completely and asked,
"Goldie, are you OK?"

"Surely, I enjoy our journey,
But sometimes, Silver, I start to worry,
And sometimes I start to despair.
Will we ever get to Pretty Bayou?
Will we ever arrive *there?*"

Silver paused and smiled,
And then she smiled again.
Then she rubbed him on the scales
And kissed him on his gills.
"Don't fret about the destination, Goldie,
And let it spoil your journey.
For Pretty Bayou isn't north or south,
East or west,
Next week or next year."

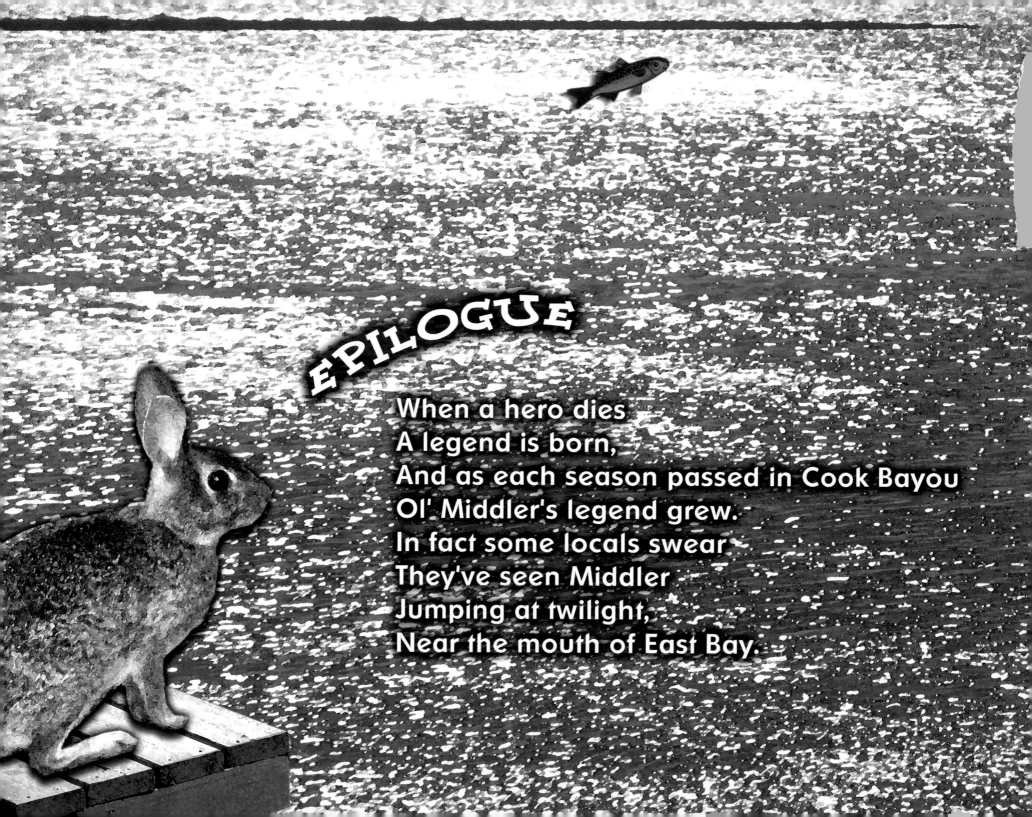

EPILOGUE

When a hero dies
A legend is born,
And as each season passed in Cook Bayou
Ol' Middler's legend grew.
In fact some locals swear
They've seen Middler
Jumping at twilight,
Near the mouth of East Bay.

And legend now has it
That when Mama Osprey
Dropped her prey
In the nest,
When it was just three seconds
From being *Too Late*,
Middler made one last desperate leap,
And two osprey chicks
Went hungry that day.

Goldie's Search for Silver

Written by
Timothy A. Weeks

Illustrator: Miss Jeanne
Illustrator and Design: Lala Rascic
Photography: Timothy A. Weeks
Editor: Kimberlee S. Bryant

ISBN 978-0-9779928-2-9
First Edition
Published by Foolosophy Media™ 2009

Foolosophy Media
1528 Primrose Lane,
Panama City, Florida, 32404
(850) 819-5623
(850) 871-2304
wisemullet@gmail.com

foolosophy™

Printed in the USA
by BookMasters